KT-385-056
DOUBLE TROUBLE
FOR ANNA HIBISCUS!
ATINUKE
LAUREN TOBIA

Anna Hibiscus
lives in Africa.
Amazing Africa.

"Anna Hibiscus,"
Papa whispers.
"Come and see..."

"Babies!" says Anna. "Two babies!"

"Your brothers, Anna Hibiscus."
Mama smiles.

"It is brothers," Anna Hibiscus tells her cousins.

"That big bump was brothers."

"Boys!" shouts Benz.

"Two boys!" whispers Angel.

"That means trouble!" says Clarity.

"Big Trouble!" says Chocolate.

"Uh-oh," thinks Anna Hibiscus.

Anna Hibiscus runs back to Mama
for her morning cuddle.

"Mama is sleeping now," whispers Papa.
"Your brothers have worn her out!"

"Uh-oh," thinks Anna Hibiscus again.
"Maybe they are trouble."

Anna Hibiscus goes down to the kitchen
for breakfast. Anna Hibiscus always
has ogi for breakfast. Uncle Bizi Sunday always
makes it for her.
But Uncle Bizi Sunday is busy.
Busy making food for Anna's mother.

"She is now eating for three!"
Uncle Bizi Sunday says.

"They *are* trouble,"
thinks Anna Hibiscus.

Anna Hibiscus takes a big ripe banana.
She goes to Grandmother's mat.
Anna Hibiscus always eats breakfast
with Grandmother.

But Grandmother is busy sleeping.

"Grandmother was up all night,"
whispers Joy.

"Helping your brothers to be born,"
whispers Common Sense.

"More trouble!"
thinks Anna Hibiscus.

Anna Hibiscus goes outside to eat her banana.
The aunties are outside. They always wash clothes
in the morning, and they always let Anna Hibiscus help.

But the aunties are not washing clothes!
They are busy rocking the babies.

"Shh..." they whisper.

"It's not easy getting babies to sleep,"
whispers Auntie Grace.

"Trouble again!" shouts Anna Hibiscus.
She shouts so loudly
the babies start to cry.

Anna Hibiscus runs to hide
before the aunties can be cross with her.

Anna Hibiscus is lonely hiding.
She thinks of the uncles.
The uncles always have time to play.

But the uncles are busy too!

"Those brothers of yours have given us a lot to do!" says Uncle Habibi.

"Double the work," says Uncle Tunde.

"Double trouble!" shouts Anna Hibiscus.

Anna Hibiscus starts to cry.

"Wha' happen?" Papa asks.

"Everybody is busy with Double Trouble!"
cries Anna Hibiscus.
"Nobody has time for me."

"Double trouble?" Papa asks.

"Those babies!"
says Anna Hibiscus.
"Those brothers!"

Papa laughs!
"You will have to share us with your
brothers, Anna," he says.

"But it's not fair!"
cries Anna Hibiscus.

"Anna Hibiscus!"
It is Uncle Bizi Sunday calling.
"Your ogi is ready now!"

"Anna!" Grandmother is calling too.
"I am waiting to eat with you!"

"We are going to need your help
with the washing, Anna Hibiscus,"
the aunties say.

"Then we will take you
to the water park."
The uncles smile. "All of you!"

"Hooray!"
shout all the cousins.
"Hurry, Anna!"

"You see." Papa smiles.
"Everybody has time
for Anna Hibiscus!"

Anna Hibiscus smiles too.

Then she looks at her brothers.
They are still crying.

Anna Hibiscus kisses one brother.
"Don't cry, little Trouble," she says.

Anna Hibiscus kisses the other brother.
"Don't cry, little Double," she says.

"We have Mama and Papa,
and Grandmother and Grandfather,
and so many aunties and uncles
and cousins to share!
You don't need to cry."

Anna Hibiscus is
so happy now!

She is going to eat ogi
with Grandmother,
splash with her aunties,
and play with her uncles
and cousins.

But first Anna Hibiscus
runs to her mother.

"Are you busy?"
Anna Hibiscus asks.

"Busy cuddling you, Anna Hibiscus,"
her mother says.

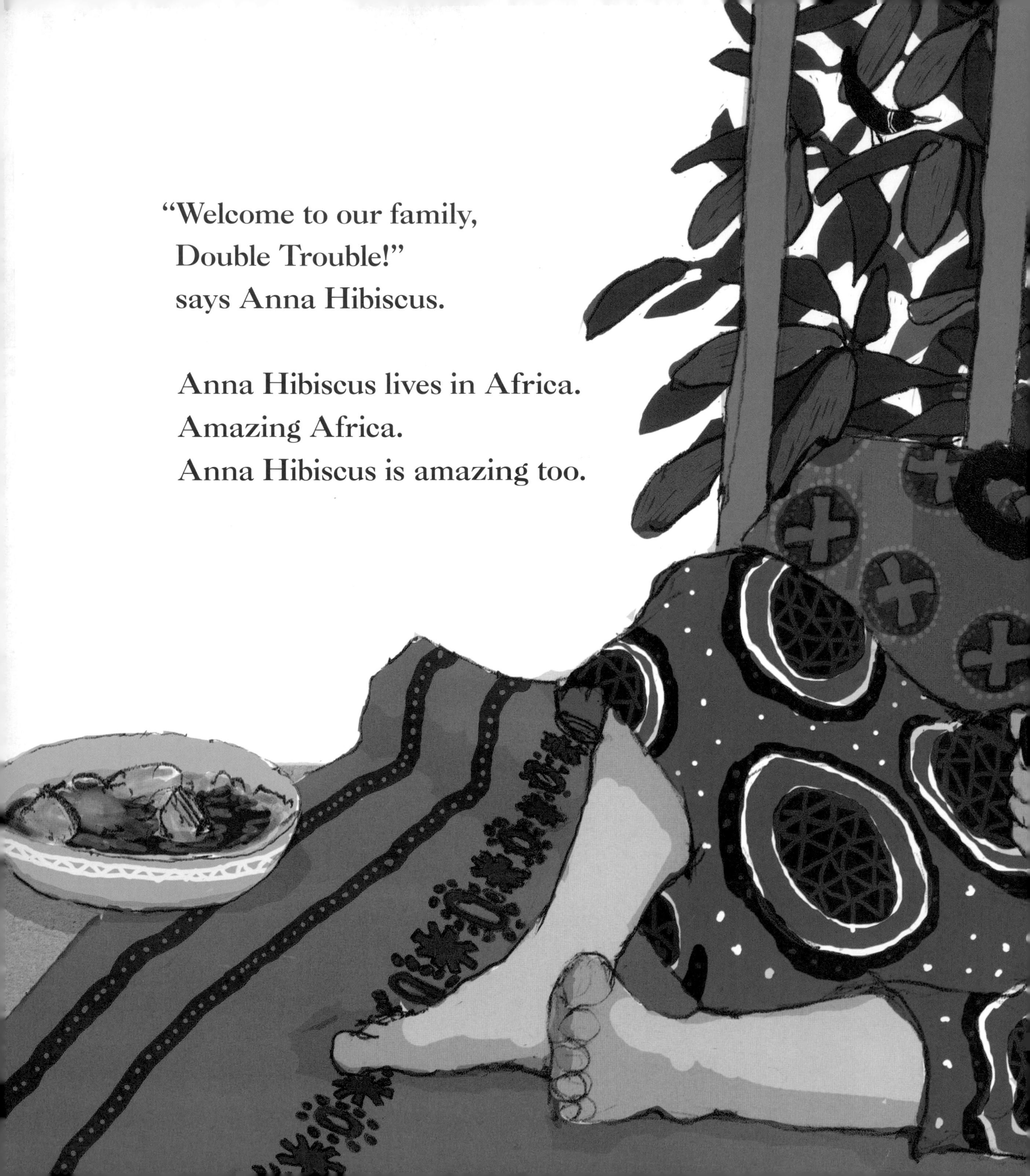

"Welcome to our family,
Double Trouble!"
says Anna Hibiscus.

Anna Hibiscus lives in Africa.
Amazing Africa.
Anna Hibiscus is amazing too.

For everyone at Little Tiger,
friends and family . . .
A very BIG thank you - J L

LITTLE TIGER PRESS
1 The Coda Centre,
189 Munster Road, London SW6 6AW
www.littletiger.co.uk

First published in Great Britain 2016



A CIP catalogue record for this book is available from the British Library

 • ISBN 978-1-84869-275-6

Printed in China • LTP/1400/1432/0216

2 4 6 8 10 9 7 5 3 1

Jonny Lambert

# THE GREAT AAA-OOO!

LITTLE TIGER PRESS
London

As Mouse scampered homeward through the dark, rackety wood, a horrible howl was heard.

AAA-OOOO!

AAA-OOOO!

Owl winked one beady eye.
"Tu-whit tu-whoo, was that you?"

"Not I," squeaked Mouse nervously.
"I . . . I . . . I thought it was you!"

"Twaddle, not I!" hooted Owl.
"If it was not you, then who,
tu-whit tu-whoo, is making this
awful **AAA-OOO?"**

AAA-OOO!
OOO!

Bear grumbled up the tree, disturbed from his slumber by the hullabaloo.
"Grrumph!" he grizzled. "Which one of you made that awful AAA-OOO?"

"Not I!" Owl huffed. "I hoot and toot and tu-whit tu-whoo."

"Nor I!" squeaked Mouse. "I scritch and scratch, squeak and chew, but never ever do I AAA-OOO!"

AAA-Ooo!
A-Ooo!

KNOCK, SMACK, THWACK, Moose tapped on the tree. "Hey, you up there ... yes you ... you three! Are you making that horrible howl?"

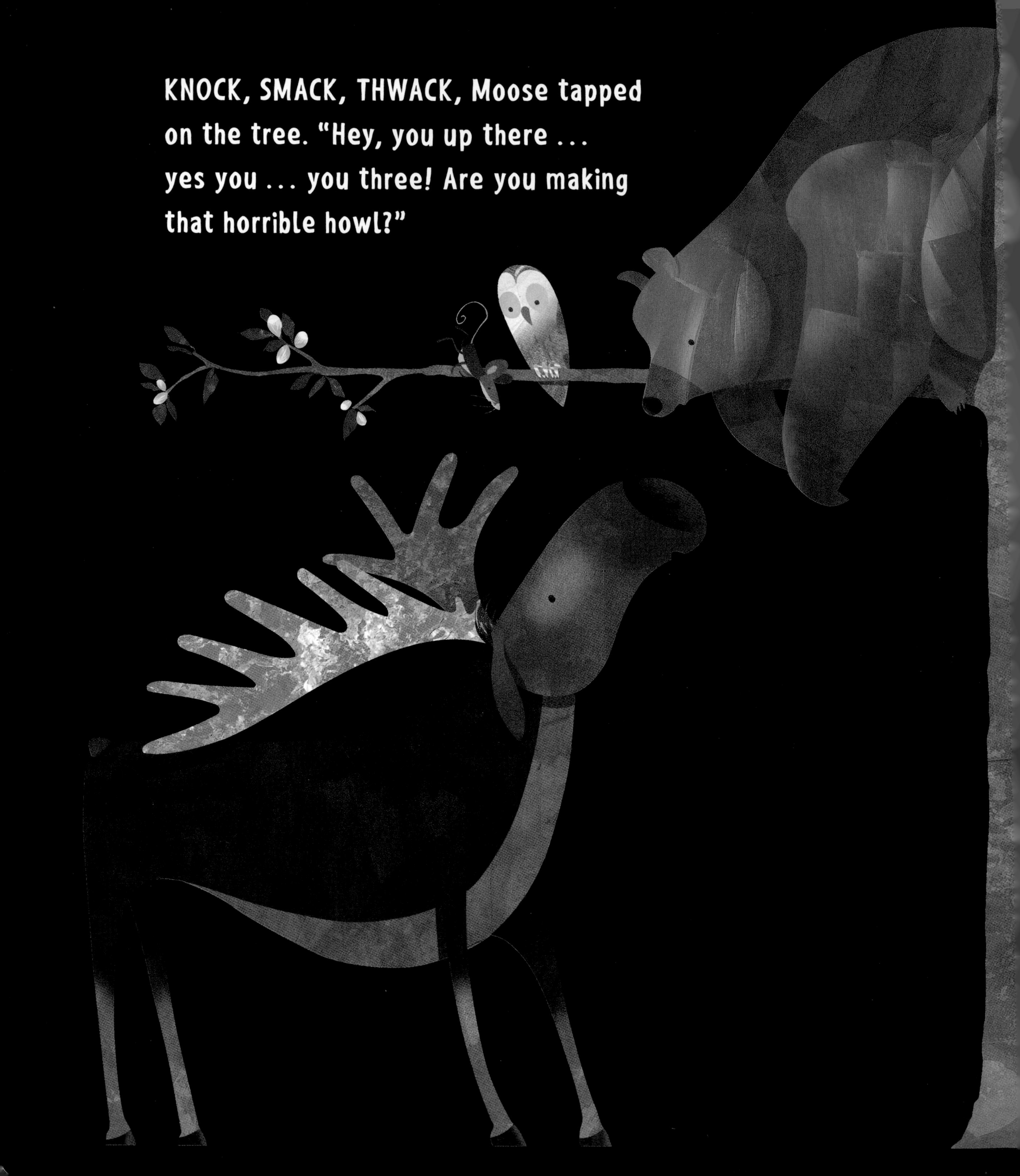

"Not us," grunted Bear. "We growl, squeak and tu-whit tu-whoo, but never ever do we AAA-OOO!"

"Then WHO?" bellowed Moose. "WHO!" Closer and louder came the awful ...

AAA-OOO!

AAA-OOO!

AAA-OOO!

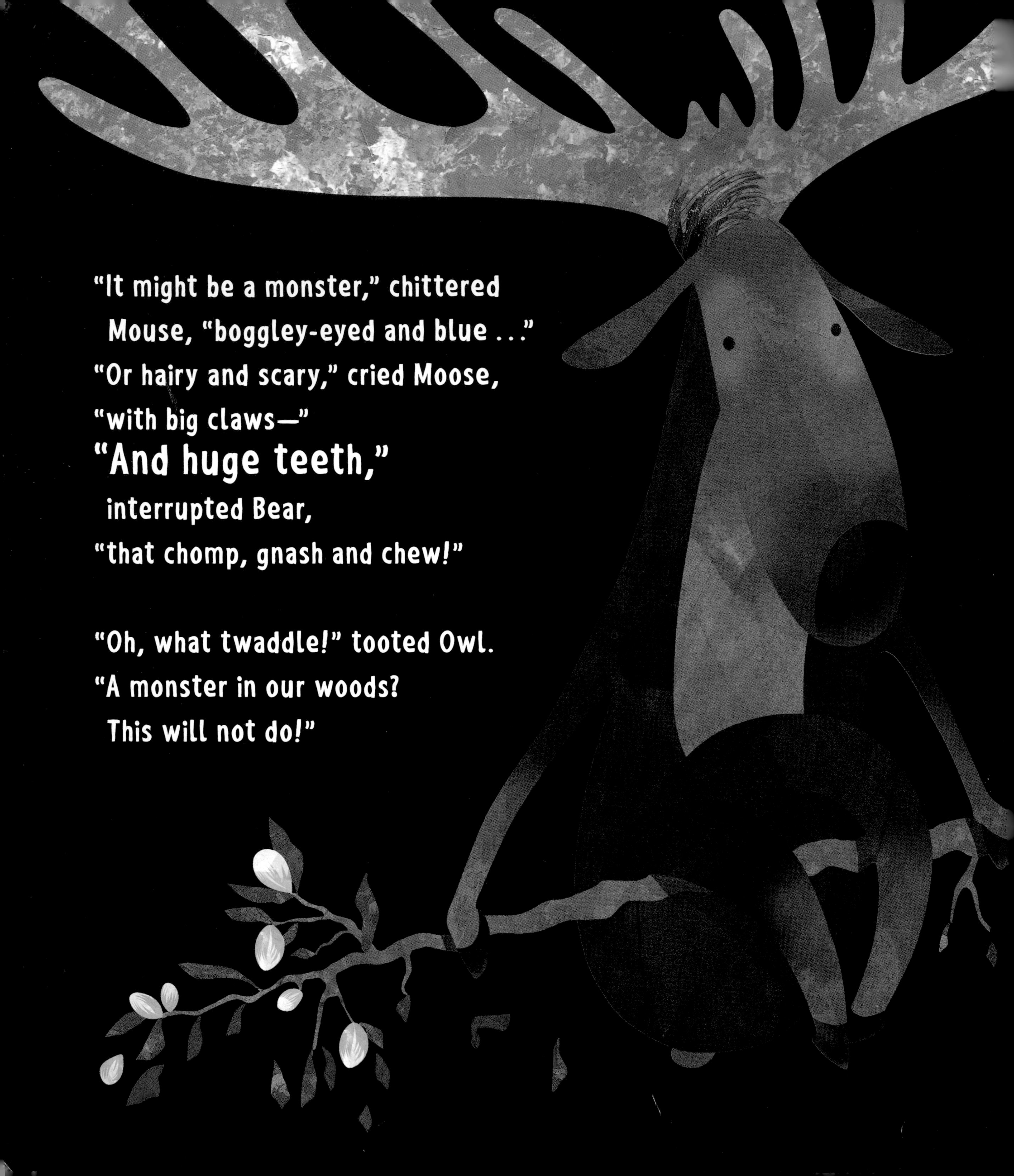

"It might be a monster," chittered
Mouse, "boggley-eyed and blue ..."
"Or hairy and scary," cried Moose,
"with big claws—"
**"And huge teeth,"**
interrupted Bear,
"that chomp, gnash and chew!"

"Oh, what twaddle!" tooted Owl.
"A monster in our woods?
This will not do!"

AAA-OOO!
AAA-OOO!

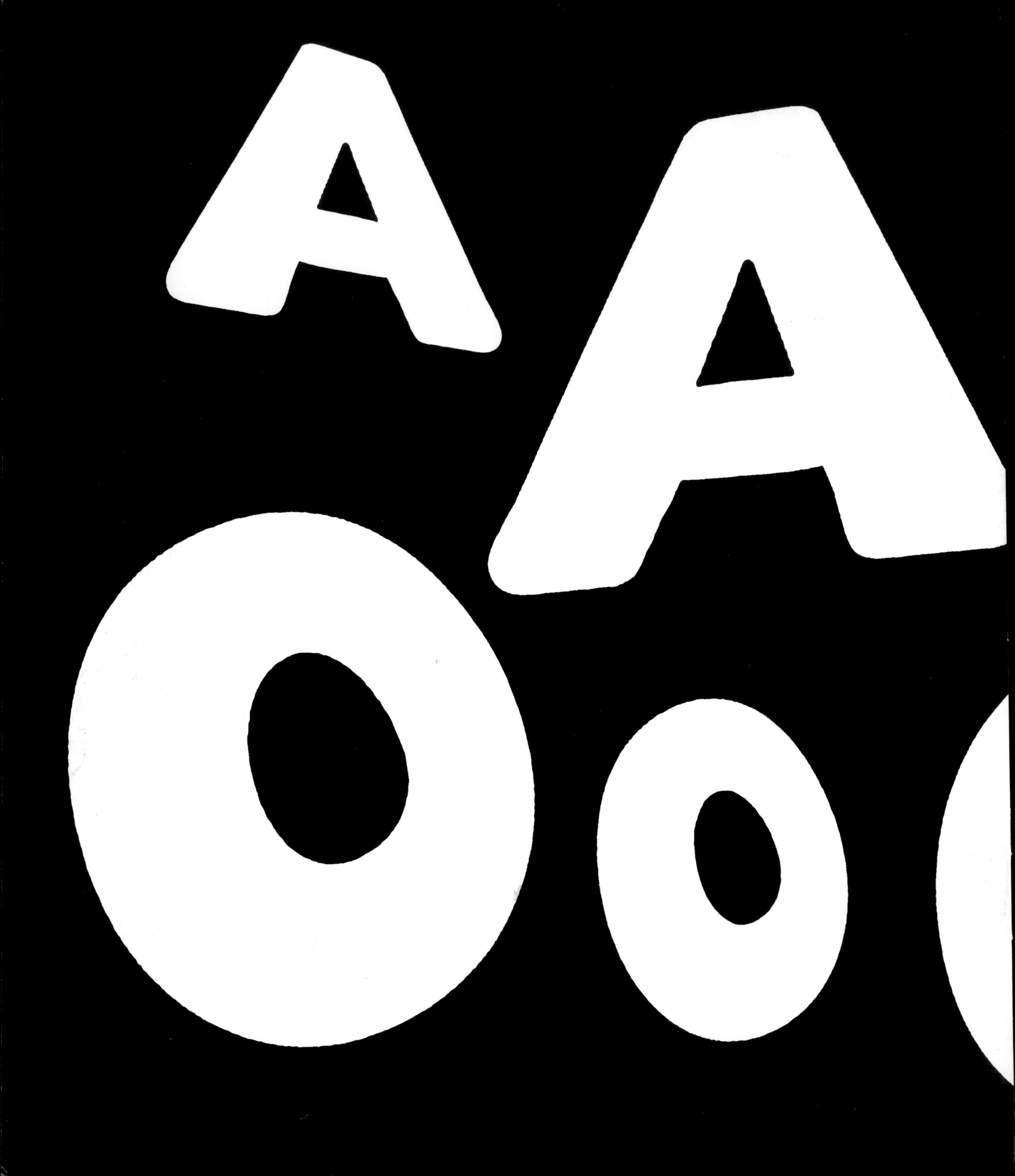

AAA-

Ooo!

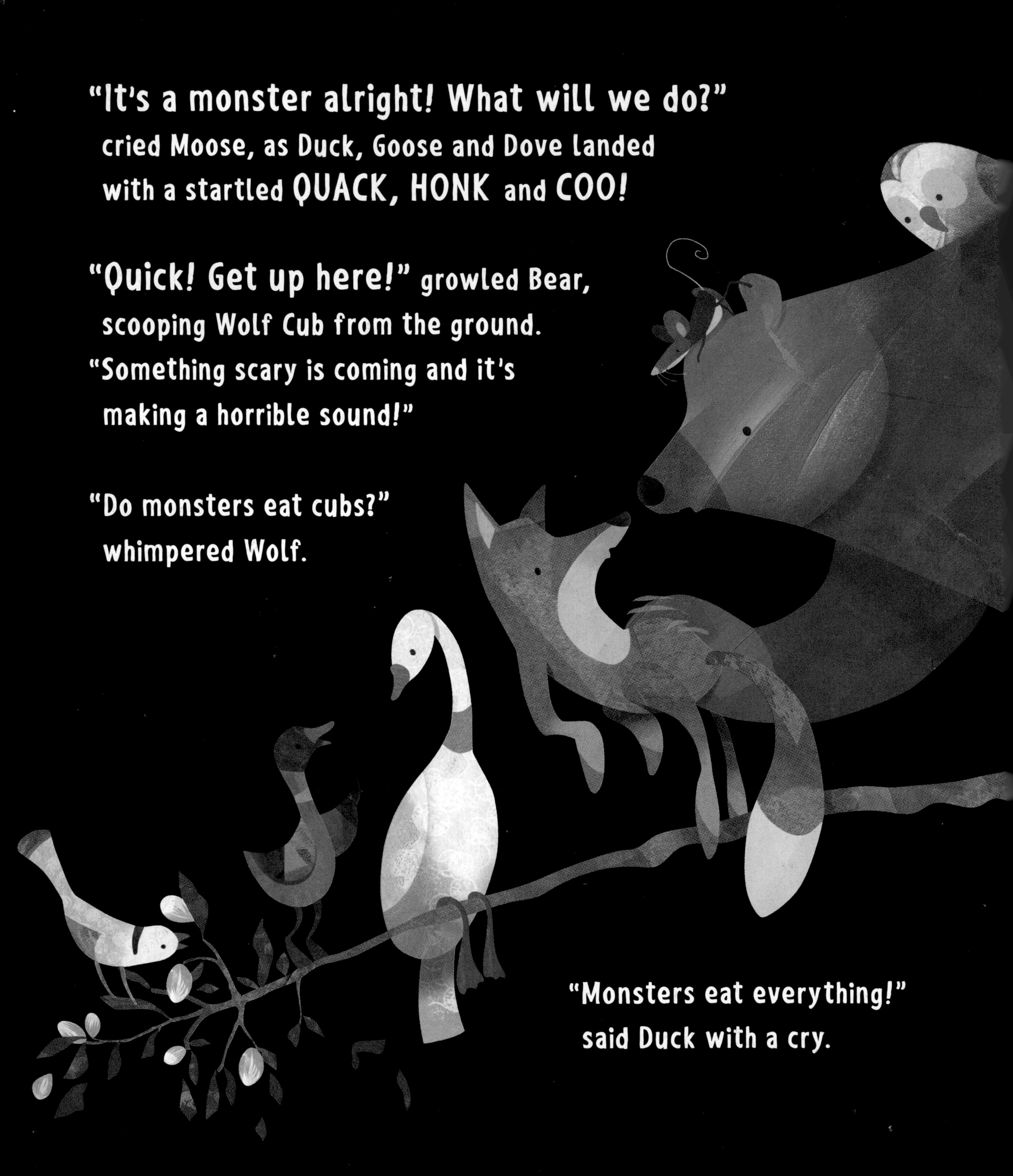

"It's a monster alright! What will we do?"
cried Moose, as Duck, Goose and Dove landed
with a startled QUACK, HONK and COO!

"Quick! Get up here!" growled Bear,
scooping Wolf Cub from the ground.
"Something scary is coming and it's
making a horrible sound!"

"Do monsters eat cubs?"
whimpered Wolf.

"Monsters eat everything!"
said Duck with a cry.

"We'll be plucked, stuffed,
and roasted, and put in a pie!"

"A pie?" roared Bear.

"Save yourselves!
Follow me!"

And the animals scrambled and clambered higher up the tree.

TWANG!
TWIST!
BEND!
Branches BUCKLED!
The tree CREAKED, SHUDDERED
and GROANED, then . . .

cra

CK!

The animals came crashing to the floor with a

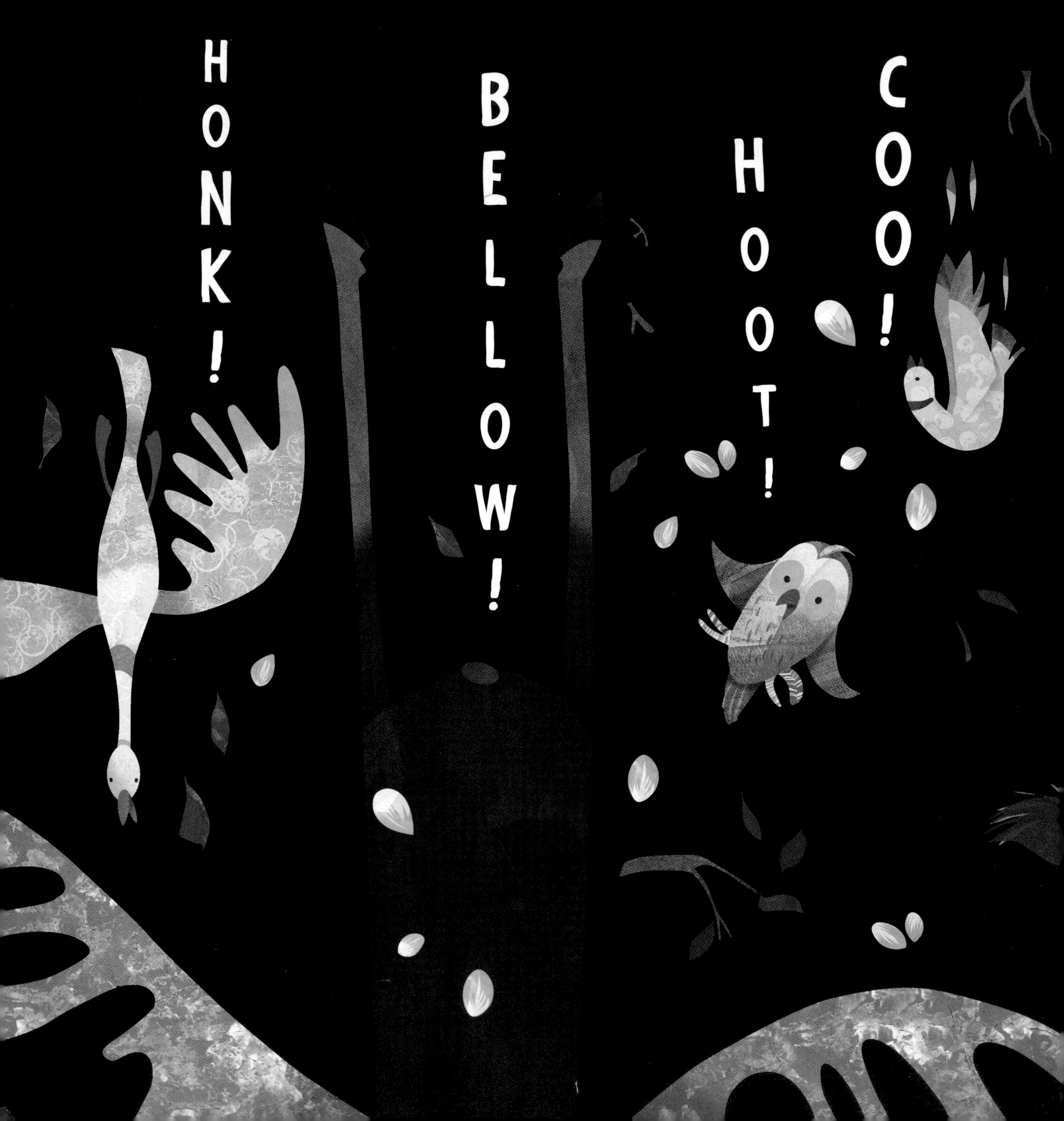

Then a THWACK!

SMACK!

SQUEAK!

And an awful AAA-OOO!

"WOLF!
It was you!" hooted Owl.
"You who made that horrible howl!"

"I'm sorry," whined Wolf.
"I didn't mean to give you
a fright. But when I'm alone
in the dark, rackety wood,
it's really SCARY at night."

Bear gave Wolf Cub a **mighty** hug.

"There, there ... it's alright.
If you promise to be quiet,
you can sleep with us tonight."

At long last, the rackety wood was peaceful once more. The animals drifted off to sleep with a . . .

**SNUFFLE, WHEEZE, SNORE . . .**

**SPLUTTER, MUTTER, GRUMBLE, COO,**

**MUMBLE, MURMUR . . .**

cock-a-d